# LENNY AND MEL

by Erik P. Kraft

Simon & Schuster Books for Young Readers

New York   London   Toronto   Sydney   Singapore

# To Anna

SIMON & SCHUSTER BOOKS FOR YOUNG READERS
An imprint of Simon & Schuster Children's Publishing Division
1230 Avenue of the Americas, New York, New York 10020

Book design by Greg Stadnyk
The text for this book is set in 15-point Berkeley Book.
The illustrations are rendered in pen and ink.
Printed in the United States of America
10 9 8 7 6 5 4 3 2 1

Library of Congress Cataloging-in-Publication Data
Kraft, Erik P.
Lenny and Mel / by Erik P. Kraft.
p. cm.
Summary: Twin brothers observe a year's worth of holidays in some very unusual ways.
ISBN 0-689-84173-6
[1. Holidays—Fiction. 2. Twins—Fiction. 3. Brothers-Fiction. 4. Schools—Fiction. 5. Humorous stories.] I. Title.
PZ7.K85843 Le 2002
[Fic]—dc21
2001032768

# CONTENTS

# Haikooties

✤✤✤

It was Labor Day, the last day of summer vacation, and Lenny and Mel knew what that meant.

It meant that once school began, they would have to be on their best behavior. So they decided to get all their worst behavior out of their system.

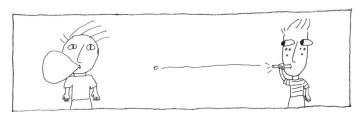

They shot spit wads at each other. They said "ain't." And they chewed gum, knowing full well that they didn't have enough for everyone.

"Boy, I feel better," said Mel.

"Me too," said Lenny. "Now we're ready to be good students."

"Especially this year, since we have Ms. Handsaw," said Mel.

"I heard she's the meanest teacher in school," said Lenny.

"I wonder what they call her to make fun," said Mel.

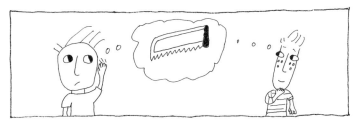

"Well," said Lenny, "instead of worrying about that, we need to think of how to make a good first impression."

"Oh," said Mel. "Maybe we should get to school before everyone else and make sure that everything is ready for when class starts. That way, we can beat everyone else to being teacher's pet."

"Good idea," said Lenny.

"And wearing ties can't hurt," said Mel.

The boys got there early enough the next morning that neither the teacher nor the other students had arrived yet. To ready themselves for the rigors of good studenthood, they had made their own lunches the night before.

"Hey!" said Lenny when they got to their homeroom. "We should have brought the teacher a gift. That's what good students do. What do you have in your lunch?"

"Why my lunch? What's wrong with your lunch?" asked Mel.

"You look better if we use yours. I'm trying to help you out," said Lenny. "Give me an apple."

"I don't have an apple," said Mel.

"Do you have *any* fruit?" asked Lenny.

"I've got ants on a log," said Mel.

"What?" said Lenny.

"Ants on a log," said Mel.

"What?" said Lenny.

"Celery with peanut butter and raisins," said Mel.

"Oh," said Lenny. "Well, give her that, then."

So they took out one log, ants and all, and put it on Ms. Handsaw's desk.

The boys took their seats.

"What can we do to make better use of our time?" Lenny asked.

"I bet those erasers haven't been clapped since June," said Mel.

So the boys clapped all the erasers until every last bit of chalk dust was out of them.

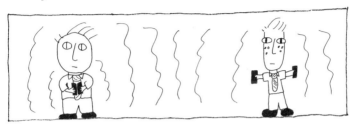

"What happened in here?" coughed Ms. Handsaw as she walked into the room.

"We got here early and clapped all the erasers," said Mel.

"We wanted to set a good example," said Lenny.

"Hmmph," said Ms. Handsaw.

"What's this?" Ms. Handsaw asked, holding up something small and white. The boys then realized that they had forgotten to cover their present during the eraser clapping.

"Ants on a log," said Lenny, "in the snow."

"Why is it on my desk?" asked Ms. Handsaw.

"We didn't have an apple," said Mel.

"Take your seats, boys," said Ms. Handsaw grumpily. "Sit quietly until the other students arrive."

The other students began to wander in. When Art Bunkleheimer arrived, he placed an enormous apple on Ms. Handsaw's desk. Then he turned so she couldn't see and stuck his tongue out at Lenny and Mel.

"He had the same idea!" gasped Mel.

Both of the boys were about to retaliate,
until they realized that truly good students
did not stick their tongue out at others.

"All right, class," Ms. Handsaw said
once all the students had arrived. "To start
off the new year, we're all going to write
haikus about what we did for our summer
vacation."

Mel groaned silently. Lenny shut his
eyes, then he rolled them. Art
Bunkleheimer scribbled away wildly.

"You have five minutes to finish," said
Ms. Handsaw.

"I'm done," said Art Bunkleheimer.

"Well!" said Ms. Handsaw excitedly. "Why don't you write a few more, then?"

Both Lenny and Mel stared at the pieces of paper in front of them. No words came to their heads. But they each started moving their pencil around to look busy.

"Time's up," said Ms. Handsaw. "Put your pencils down. Who would like to read theirs?"

Art Bunkleheimer's hand shot up. Lenny looked at his paper. On it he had drawn a picture of a monkey cooking hamburgers on a grill. Mel's paper had only a few lines and a star scrawled on it. But they both raised their hands, just to keep up with Art.

"Mr. Bunkleheimer, you may go first," said Ms. Handsaw.

Art stood up. "I just don't know which one to read, they're all so good." Then after a moment of thought he said, "I'll read the first one.

*"I spent the whole time*
*Waiting to meet the brand-new*
*Wonderful teacher."*

*Bleah,* thought the boys.
"*Very* good, Art," said Ms. Handsaw, smiling. Then she stopped smiling and said, "Lenny, it's your turn."

Lenny stood up, looked at his drawing, and began to speak:

*"Baboon barbecue*
*Grilling burgers on my lawn*
*Medium rare, please."*

"Hmmph," hmmphed Ms. Handsaw. "I'm not so sure about that one."
Mel began to panic.
"Mel, now you may read us yours."
Mel looked at the mess on his paper. Now he wanted more than ever to be a good student, but it seemed like the end was near. He took a deep breath and spoke:

*"Look at the big star*
*Watch it swirl about the sky*
*Now I'm back at school."*

"Hmm. Well, that was actually quite nice, Mel," said Ms. Handsaw.

Mel breathed a sigh of relief.

"Now, everyone hand in your poems to me," said Ms. Handsaw, and she began to walk around the room, picking up the pieces of paper from the children's desks.

Mel grabbed his pencil. "What did I say? What did I say?" But Lenny didn't answer. He was too busy trying to write down his baboon haiku before Ms. Handsaw got to his desk.

# Hallowieners

🎃 🎃 🎃

Halloween was a smashing success. Not for Lenny and Mel, though. Their costumes were the problem. Lenny had taped candy

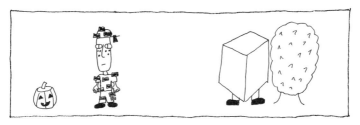

wrappers all over himself and gone as the floor of the movie theater. Mel had cut holes for his legs in a box and gone as a box. He had forgotten to cut holes for his eyes, however, and did a lot of walking into trees and telephone poles. Lenny spent most of the night biting his tongue when people said, "Oh, you're Trash Day!" Mel spent most of the night fighting his way out of shrubs.

"Show me where to go," said Mel, crashing into a yard gnome. "I can't see."

"I've got problems of my own," said Lenny. The tape he had used wasn't very good, and he was in constant danger of leaving a trail of Zagnut wrappers behind him.

"Hey, Trash Day! My lawn's not part of your costume!" someone yelled out a window.

"Sorry," Lenny shouted as he picked up the mess.

"And easy on the yard gnome!"

"Huh?" said Mel, crashing into the gnome again.

"Get away from there," said Lenny, shoving Mel away from the gnome.

"Next year I'm going as a yard gnome and I'm going to stand on this guy's lawn all night," said Mel as the boys headed for home.

Fortunately all the candy they had unwrapped for Lenny's costume was waiting for them when they got back.

# The Leftover Fairy

It was the week after Thanksgiving, and Lenny and Mel were sick.

"I'm sick of eating turkey," said Lenny.

"Me too," said Mel. "This is worse than Easter. All those eggs in the back of the refrigerator must have hatched into turkeys."

They had eaten turkey soup, turkey pot pies, hot open-faced turkey sandwiches, turkey tetrazzini, turkey pea wiggle, turkey with rice, turkey pizza, and turkey pitas, and they had washed it all down with cool turkey frappes.

"Mom says every cloud has a silver lining," said Lenny, sipping a frappe. "There must be some way to turn all this turkey into a profit."

"You're right," said Mel. "We should leave it for the Leftover Fairy."

"The what?" asked Lenny.

"The Leftover Fairy," said Mel. "At night the Leftover Fairy sails through the air in his gravy boat, collecting leftovers. He pays a dollar a pound."

"Who told you this?" asked Lenny.

"Fast Eddie, in my gym class," said Mel.

"He said that he made enough to buy a bike with all his fruitcakes from last Christmas."

"So, what do we do?" asked Lenny.

"It's just like the tooth fairy," said Mel. "We just put all the leftovers under our pillows, and the next morning, *whammo!* We're rolling in booty."

"Let's use your bed," said Lenny.

That night, just before bedtime, Lenny and Mel went to the refrigerator and gathered up all the leftovers.

"What's going on in there?" their mother asked.

"Mmm. Boy am I hungry," said Lenny.

"Mmm. Me too," said Mel.

"Don't eat in bed," their mother said. "You'll get ants."

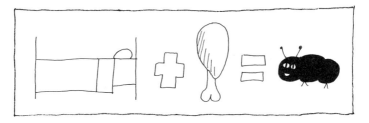

They piled up all the leftovers under Mel's pillow.

"That's a big pile," said Lenny.

"I think I'll sleep on the couch," said Mel.

The next morning the boys found a bloated and hairy thing lying on its back on the floor of Mel's bedroom. It had a drumstick hanging out of its mouth.

"We've killed the fairy!" shouted Mel.

"No, we didn't, that's Ahab!" exclaimed
Lenny

"We've killed the cat!" shouted Mel.

"No, Ahab will be okay," said Lenny. "He
eats Mom's shepherd's pie all the time and
lives. And he ate only about twenty dollars'
worth of the leftovers."

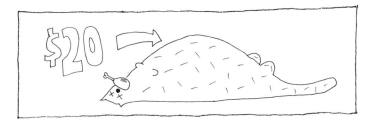

Mel hung his head in shame. "I jinxed it by not sleeping with the leftovers. Tonight we'll get the money."

That night as he slept, Mel dreamed that the Leftover Fairy was sprinkling him with his special magic croutons. He felt all tingly as he slept.

When he woke up, he was covered with ants.

"Help!" he shouted.

Lenny and their mother ran into the room.

"You kids have ruined these leftovers,"

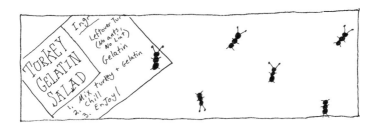

said their mother. "I can't make turkey gelatin salad with leftovers that are covered with ants and lint. No more turkey for you kids until next Thanksgiving."

Lenny and Mel were ecstatic.

"Well, he may have cheated us out of the money," said Mel, "but we were certainly blessed by the Leftover Fairy."

# Christmas Cheese

🧦 🧦 🧦

"If we're going to get anything good this year, we had better leave Santa the right snack," said Lenny.

"Like waffles?" asked Mel.

"Waffles will get cold," said Lenny. "Santa comes late."

"How about roast beef?"

"Santa's a vegetarian," said Lenny. "That way, the reindeer don't think he's going to eat them."

"Oh," said Mel. "That makes sense."

The boys thought and thought. What

was something Santa would like as much
as they did?

"*Cheese!*" they both shouted.

They ran to the refrigerator. "Hey, there
are two kinds in here," said Lenny.

"What are they?" asked Mel.

"Well, we've got those slices, and then
there's a chunk of"—he read slowly—
"ja-la-peñ-o."

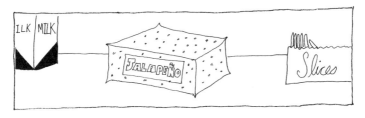

"What's that?" asked Mel.

"I think it means 'super cheese,'" said
Lenny.

"Well, let's give that to Santa, and then

we can give each of the reindeer a slice, so they don't feel left out," said Mel.

The boys gathered up the cheese and put it on the mantel, with a note on the jalapeño hunk that said, FOR SANTA, and a note next to the slices that said, FOR THE REINDEER.

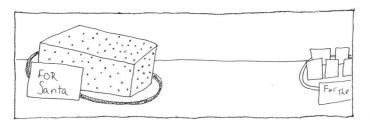

"Not very exciting," said Lenny, looking at the cheese display.

"Let's put some lights on it," said Mel, and they began to take lights off the Christmas tree and wrap them around the cheese.

"That's better," said Mel, staring into the lights.

"Yeah, but not Christmassy enough," said Lenny. He broke a few twigs off of the tree and stuck them in the cheese. Mel hung a few ornaments on them.

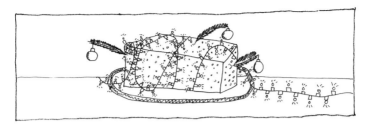

"Now, that's a good snack," said Lenny.

The boys could hardly sleep that night, the excitement was too much. Lenny dreamed about the inflatable boat he wanted Santa to bring. Mel dreamed of a big breakfast of waffles.

When morning came, the boys ran downstairs. The cheese was gone and there was a note waiting for them.

*Dear Lenny and Mel,*

    *Your snack for me was so fancy, I decided it was too nice to eat. I'm going to use it as a hood*

ornament for my sleigh instead. My old one was stolen by some prankster elves, and they haven't given it back. Don't ask what they got in their stockings this year. Such a nice gift from you boys deserves some nice gifts in return. By that I mean the gifts you asked for. I'll give the socks and underwear to someone else this year.

     *Merry Christmas,*

     *Santa*

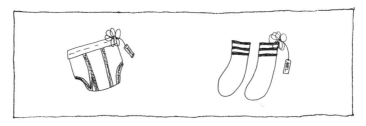

"A cheese hood ornament? That's kind of gross," said Mel.

"Shhh! He'll hear you!" said Lenny.

"You mean he still watches, even on

Christmas Day?" asked Mel. "I thought he'd take a day off."

"That's how he gets you," said Lenny. "A whole bunch of people get on the naughty list right off the bat."

"Man, Santa's sneaky," said Mel. Then the boys walked over to the Christmas tree to inflate their presents.

# Dropping the Ball

"So, how do they know it's New Year's?" Lenny asked his father.

"Well, that's when the ball drops," he answered.

"What?" said Mel.

"In New York there's a ball on top of a building, and when it drops, then it's a new year," their father clarified.

Lenny pictured someone kicking a soccer ball off the roof.

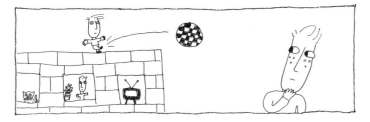

Mel thought about the people in the top-floor apartment of that building. What

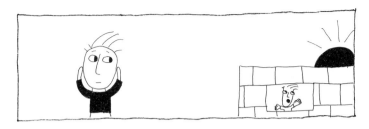

a ruckus it would make when the ball hit.

A little while later Mel asked, "Does the ball drop at the same time every year?"

"Yes, they even show it on TV," their father said.

"Can we watch it?"

"If you can stay up that late. When I was your age, I'd try and I'd always fall asleep. It was four years before I managed to stay up and actually see it."

"Why didn't you tape it?" Lenny asked.

Their father went into a lengthy explanation about how they didn't have VCRs when he was a boy, and you always had to be home to watch the shows you wanted to see, and blah, blah, blah, on and on. The boys politely watched their father talk, nodded occasionally to make it seem like they were listening, and thought about ways they could make themselves stay awake.

They decided to put a mutual pinching system in place.

Starting at eight o'clock the boys sat side by side in front of the TV and took turns pinching each other to prevent their falling asleep. As an unplanned bonus, they each ended up saying "ow," which also helped the staying-awake process.

"Ow."

"Ow."

"Ow."

"Ow."

"What's going on in there?" their father yelled from the other room.

"We're waiting for the ball to drop," said Lenny.

"Well, you've still got a while," said their father.

The boys were willing to wait. And wait. And wait.

Finally they showed the ball on TV.

It was not what the boys had expected.

Rather than a soccer ball, or something useful, it was a giant ball covered in tiny white lights. It sat on top of a pole that had

a clock in front of it, counting down the
time until the new year.

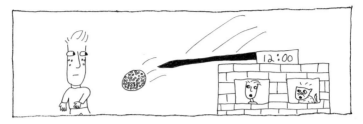

Lenny imagined the pole tipping over
and dropping the ball into the crowd
below, which made him a little queasy.
Surely there was a better way to let people
know a new year had begun.

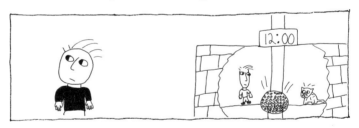

Mel imagined the ball sliding down the
pole, right through the roof and all the way
down to the basement, like a fireman.

Unknown to either of the boys, the
pinching had begun to slow down.

Then it got slower still.

Then it stopped.

"Hey, guys! Wake up! You're going to miss it!" their father was yelling.

The boys opened their eyes. Even with such an exciting event taking place, it sure was hard to wake up.

The ball slowly slid down the pole as the crowd counted down from ten. It stopped at the bottom, and the crowd let out a tremendous cheer.

"That's it?" said a sleepy Lenny.

"Happy New Year," said Mel, who had already closed his eyes again. Lenny would have pinched him to wake him up, but he was too busy falling back asleep himself.

Their father covered them with a blanket. "Happy New Year, boys," he said as he shut off the light.

# Dog-Day Afternoon

♡ ♡ ♡

"What's this?" asked Art Bunkleheimer.

"A valentine," said Lenny.

Art looked at the piece of paper with a dog drawn on it. WE LOVE VALENTINE, it said.

"What's this got to do with me?" he asked.

"It's not about you," said Mel. "It's Valentine's Day."

The rest of the students were as confused as Art was.

"What's all the grumbling about, class?" asked Ms. Handsaw.

Angelina Rosenschontz raised her hand. "Lenny and Mel's valentines are for a dog," she said.

Ms. Handsaw looked at one of the valentines. "And an ugly one at that," she said. "Lenny and Mel, can you explain this?"

"Well, Valentine is our dog," said Lenny.

"And we love him," said Mel.

"And it's Valentine's Day," said Lenny.

"I think you boys are trying to get out of appreciating your classmates," said Ms. Handsaw.

"But every dog must have its day," said
Lenny.

"That's not really what that means," said
Ms. Handsaw.

"Well, what does it mean?" asked Mel.

Ms. Handsaw thought for a minute.
"Well, it doesn't mean anything about your
weird-looking dog."

"Why can't we share our love for
Valentine today?" asked Lenny.

"Isn't sharing good?" asked Mel.

"Sometimes it's not the right time to
share something," said Ms. Handsaw.

"Oh," said Mel, "like when Valentine has drooled on it."

"Could you stop thinking about Valentine for a minute?" said Ms. Handsaw.

"But it's Valentine's Day," said Lenny.

"I'm confused," said Mel.

"Valentine's Day is for you to show your love for your fellow students."

"We did," said Lenny.

"We showed them how much we love Valentine by making these cards," said Mel.

"I said show your love *for* them, not show your love *to* them."

"You mean we should hug and kiss them?" asked Lenny.

"Bleah," said Mel. "What an awful holiday."

"No kissing in school," said Ms.

Handsaw. "You show your love by making them cards."

"We did," said Lenny.

"Your card should say something like, 'Dear Art Bunkleheimer, I love you.'"

"You love Art Bunkleheimer?" asked Mel.

"No, that's what your card might say," said Ms. Handsaw.

"I don't love that guy," said Lenny. "He gave me a wedgie in gym."

Ms. Handsaw had had enough. "You boys are wasting class time," she said. "I'll let your teacher next year try to explain it to you. Now, take your seats."

"Do you think she knows we know what she means?" Mel whispered to Lenny.

"Who cares?" said Lenny. "As long as we don't have to tell Art we love him."

# Head to the Chief

⠰⠳ ⠂⠆ ⠲⠄

"Lenny and Mel," said Ms. Handsaw, "your assignment will be to give a five-minute talk about Presidents' Day and what it means to us. You have a week."

"No problem," said Lenny.

"You bet," said Mel.

Later, at home that evening, the boys still felt confident.

"The key to a good presentation is costumes," said Lenny.

"You mean like a stovepipe hat?" asked Mel.

"When I say 'costumes,' I mean giant papier-mâché heads," said Lenny.

"Oh," said Mel. "My mistake. I guess we'll need to get a lot of newspaper together."

"What happened to the Sunday paper?" the boys' father asked.

"I haven't seen it," said their mother.

The boys said nothing.

"How are we going to get the heads to be big?" asked Mel.

"We'll have to blow up trash bags," said Lenny.

"Where are we going to get fireworks?" asked Mel.

"When I say 'blow up,' I mean inflate," said Lenny. "Though maybe after the presentation we can blow them up."

"When you said 'blow up' that time, you meant blow up, right?" asked Mel.

Lenny took a deep breath and tried not to say anything rude.

The boys filled plastic bags with air to cover with the papier-mâché. It took a lot of blowing. "The bigger the head, the better the grade," said Lenny.

"Has anyone seen the cover to the cat's

bed?" the boys' mother asked.

Mel said nothing as he glued a leopard-print beard to Abe Lincoln's face.

"Well, we were going to have ziti for dinner, but we seem to be out," their father said. "So I guess we'll have grilled cheese instead."

"Well, that worked out," Mel whispered to Lenny. "We get hair for George and our favorite meal."

"Anyone want to play dominoes?" their mother asked.

"Er, not right now," Lenny said, quietly gluing the last of George Washington's wooden domino teeth in place.

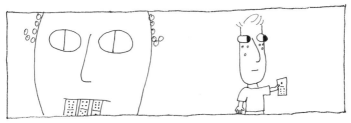

"How come his teeth have dots on them?" Mel asked.

"Everyone knows that George Washington only ate candy bars," said Lenny. "Those are cavities. That's why he never smiles."

When it came time to paint, the boys encountered a slight problem.

"We've only got pink paint," said Mel. "That stuff left over from painting the bathroom."

"Well, I guess that will have to do," said Lenny.

"They look like they're blushing," Mel said when they finished.

"That's because these heads are so good, it's embarrassing," said Lenny.

The boys stood in front of the class in their heads.

"I'm George Washington," said Lenny.

"I'm Abraham Lincoln," said Mel.

The class waited for more.

And waited.

And waited.

Lenny and Mel didn't notice that the class was staring at them in anticipation.

Having learned from Mel's Halloween experience, they had cut eyeholes. But it was still hard to see, since they had cut them in the noses instead of the eyes. And it was really hot inside the heads, so their thoughts were occupied with visions of cooler places.

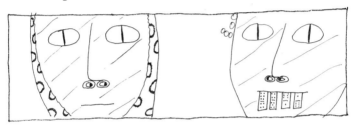

"Uh, boys," said Ms. Handsaw, "we know who you are, you've done a lovely job with these heads, but what can you tell us about Presidents' Day?"

And then the boys realized that they'd forgotten something.

"Um," said Lenny, "Presidents' Day is the day for presidents." He paused. "There are a lot of sales on this day."

Mel listened in horror as their grade slipped away. But he figured he should at least say something.

"Four score and seven years ago," he began, "I decided I didn't want to share a day with a wooden-toothed nincompoop." Then he slugged Lenny's head right in the teeth, which was really a lucky shot, since he couldn't see a thing.

"Some people think only about themselves and not about savings," Lenny shouted, mimicking what his mother always used to say on the way to buy school clothes at Discount Mart. He went to shove Mel but tripped on a desk and fell down. Then something fell on top of him. It turned out to be Mel, who had gone for a countershove and tripped over his fallen fellow president.

"Well, we really blew that one," Lenny said as they sat waiting in the principal's office.

"Yeah, but the heads looked nice," said Mel.

# Cinco de My, Oh, My

After a lunch of microwave burritos that were hot on the edges and frozen in the middle, the Cinco de Mayo party was really ready to get going.

"Lenny and Mel," Ms. Handsaw said, "did you bring the piñatas?"

"You bet," said Lenny.

Mel reached into a bag and pulled out the heads they had made for Presidents' Day.

"Um, those are interesting piñatas," said Ms. Handsaw.

"We thought it would be good to recycle them," said Mel.

"Are they at least filled with treats?" Ms. Handsaw asked.

"Of course," said Lenny.

"Well, I suppose they'll get the job done," said Ms. Handsaw.

Earl the janitor had fixed the Lincoln head to a rope, which was then tied to a rake held by his assistant, Mr. Bunster.

"Let 'er rip," said Earl.

Everyone groaned when Art Bunkleheimer was chosen to swing at the piñata first.

"But he's the best baseball player in class," said Lenny.

"It's all over if he hits it," said Mel.

"Good thing there are two piñatas."

Ms. Handsaw blindfolded Art, spun him around, and let him stagger toward victory.

*Whack!*

Mr. Bunster wasn't as fast with yanking the piñata out of the way as he should have been, and Art nailed it dead on.

Instead of smashing the piñata to pieces in a shower of candy like everyone expected, Art's hit hardly even made a dent in it.

"She's a sturdy one," said Mr. Bunster.

"Abe Lincoln is a he," said Lenny.

Mr. Bunster just looked confused.

Art was given another chance to hit the

piñata. Again he hit it dead on and the piñata barely seemed to notice.

"Take off your blindfold, Art," said Ms. Handsaw. "Children, grab some sticks. I think this is going to be a tough one."

The children scrambled to find sturdy sticks to beat the piñata with. Mr. Bunster put Abe on the ground, and the children went at him furiously. Many sticks were broken in the process, but little progress was made.

"Step aside, children," said Earl. He grabbed the rake, got a running start, and hit the head with all his strength. He managed to take a good-size chunk out of the papier-mâché fortress and walked closer to examine it.

"It's got to be a good two inches thick,"

he said. "No wonder it didn't break."

"We wanted it to be sturdy," said Mel.

Earl picked up the head to shake out the candy, but nothing fell out. He shook it and shook it, and then finally a large, lumpy brown glob fell out.

"What kind of candy is that?" asked Mr. Bunster.

"We didn't fill it with candy," said Lenny. "We filled it with raisins."

"They're better for you than candy," said Mel.

*And much, much cheaper,* thought Lenny.

Mr. Bunster looked confused again.

"Well, traditionally candy is in piñatas," said Ms. Handsaw, cautiously poking at the raisin clump with a stick. "Mr. Bunster, why don't you run to the store and buy some candy so we can keep things authentic."

"I'll keep the heads in the storeroom for the next time we need a raisin piñata," said Earl.

Lenny and Mel didn't like the idea of wasting raisins, but free candy was free candy.

# See Who Salutes

※ ※ ※

"Hey, today's Flag Day," Mel said, looking at the calendar.

"Well, we'd better get cracking, then," said Lenny. "We don't even have a flag."

The boys began rummaging through their toy box, looking for anything suitable to use as a flag.

"Hmm," said Mel. "If I were a flag, where would I be?"

"If you were a flag, you wouldn't ask these questions," said Lenny.

Mel rummaged through the box some

more. "I've got a guitar strap," said Mel.

"Not grand enough," said Lenny.

"How about a football?"

"Not flaggy enough."

The toy box proved to be a bust, so the boys went into the bathroom.

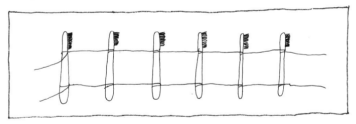

"We could tie a bunch of toothbrushes together with dental floss," said Mel.

"Too clunky," said Lenny. "A flag is supposed to soar with the wind."

"Gauze?"

"Too thin."

"A towel?"

All the towels in the bathroom had bright orange flowers printed all over them. Though the boys agreed that flowers were nice, the towels were a bit much.

"Let's try the kitchen," said Lenny.

"Paper towels?" asked Mel.

"They won't hold up against repeated wavings," said Lenny.

Mel opened the cabinet under the sink, and a bunch of grocery bags fell out onto the floor. "We could use a bag," said Mel.

"Hmm. Maybe we could," said Lenny.

"We could decorate it however we wanted," said Mel.

"Now, that's a good idea," said Lenny.

"Paper or plastic?" asked Mel.

For once, this was an easy decision.

"Paper," said Lenny.

The boys got out some paints and
markers and began to decorate the flag.
Lenny drew Mel. Mel drew Lenny. And in
honor of the towels that were a bit much to
be flags, the boys added a few tastefully
done flowers.

"Well, now what?" asked Mel.

"A parade, of course," said Lenny. "How
else are we going to show off our new
flag?"

The boys taped the paper bag to a
broom. Rock-paper-scissors decided that
Mel got to carry the flag. Lenny grabbed a

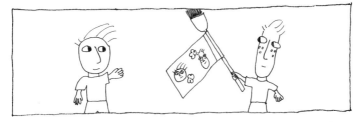

couple of pot lids for cymbals, and the parade was on.

The boys headed down the street. Lenny crashed his cymbals proudly, and Mel waved the flag like a wild man, but all that really happened was the neighbors looked out the windows to see what the ruckus was about.

"Nobody knows what's going on," said Mel. "Don't these people have calendars?"

"We need a song," said Lenny.

"You're a grand old flag, and you're made of a bag," sang Mel. "Blah blah blah,

blah blah blah, blah blah blaaaah."

Lenny crashed the cymbals.

Finally they were making enough noise for people to start asking questions.

"What's going on out there?" the lady across the street yelled, leaning out her window.

"Flag Day parade!" shouted Lenny and Mel, who had gotten a really good marching rhythm going at this point.

"Flag Day?" the lady said. "Well, I had no idea!" She pulled herself in from the window and a minute later charged out her front door waving a flowered towel tied to a wooden spoon. She got in line behind Lenny, and they marched up and down the street yelling, "Flag Day!" amid cymbal crashes. This chant got the point across

better, and soon people all up and down the street had joined in, waving sock flags, girdle flags, and one very large flag made out of an old tent.

It was the best Flag Day ever.